Mice & Spiders & Webs....Oh My!

by

Sherrill S. Cannon

Illustrations by Kalpart

Strategic Book Publishing and Rights Co.

Strategic Book Publishing and Rights Co., LLC
USA | Singapore
www.sbpra.com

For information about special discounts for bulk purchases,
please contact Strategic Book Publishing and Rights Co., LLC. Special Sales,
at bookorder@sbpra.net.

ISBN: 978-1-63135-949-1

For
Judith Conger Shaffer
Sister of my Heart
&
for my
Grandnieces
Savannah Rae & Isabel Quinn

& for my Grands:

Lindsay Alexis   Joshua Cakebread
Kelsey Beth   Parker James
Mikaila Bryn   Colby Stalker
Kylie Brenna   Tucker Flynn
Chloe Grey   Cristiano Cannon

Thank you to the illustrator of all of my books, KJ of Kalpart,
& her team of artists!

Rosemary said she would not go
to school,

No matter the law, no matter
the rule!

It was too much to ask and it
wasn't quite fair,

When school opened Monday,
she wouldn't be there!

Her mother asked, "Rosemary, what could be wrong?

You love it at school! It's where you belong.

You have lots of friends, and you're learning to read.

What else could any child possibly need?"

But Rosemary cried that her problem was grave;

She was not very strong, she was not very brave.

No matter what Mom said, she'd not leave the house;

Her teacher had warned her, she'd soon have a mouse!

She knew it was silly, she should be ashamed,

But she just couldn't help it, she sadly explained.

She didn't like mice – their noise or their smell;

They might even bite her, were dirty as well.

They frightened her, although they were quite small,

And she just couldn't help it – no, not at all.

Her mother said, "Rosemary, mice can be fun,

They have a small wheel where they run and they run.

They stay in a cage or container of glass;

You've longed for a pet – now you'll have one in class!"

"Well, maybe," said Rosie, "I might like the mouse,

But still I am sure I will not leave this house.

The mouse is not all I am frightened about,

We'll have spiders too, I also found out!"

"I know they're just bugs, and perhaps they won't bite,

But something about them just gives me a fright.

They move much too quickly, they scurry and crawl,

They just make me shudder, although they are small.

I know I should like them – I can't, though I try.

If this one has legs that are hairy, I'll cry!"

Her mother said, "Spiders? That's strange to select.

They must be a part of a science project.

Are you sure she said 'Spiders'?" Then Rosemary said,

"I'm sure she meant spiders, she spoke of their web!"

"And the worst thing," she added, "it's really not fair,

'Cause only the *girls* will have to be there!"

"Are you sure?" asked her mother. "That doesn't seem wise."

"She said 'female,'" said Rosie. "That means no guys!"

Her mother said, "This really doesn't seem right.

There must be a reason for such a big slight!

Your teacher has always been fair to you all.

You're treated alike, the big and the small,

The boys and the girls, the dark and the fair.

I'll take you to school, and meet Ms. Eddy there.

I'll talk to her, tell her what you've told me here,

And ask her to help you to cope with your fear."

So Rosie and Mom left home Monday morning,

To go see Ms. Eddy about Friday's warning.

Ms. Eddy stood smiling in front of her door,

And Rosemary's mom told her what she'd come for.

She told her of Rosemary's fear of the mouse,

How she was determined to not leave her house.

She told her that spider webs frightened Rosemary;

Both spiders and mice, she found awfully scary!

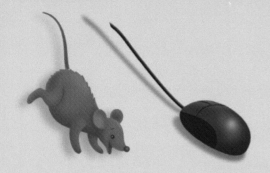

Ms. Eddy just stared, then she started to laugh,

"I think you misheard what I said to the class!

I told all the children that starting next week,

We'd have a surprise: some machines that can speak!

I thought they'd be happy to know in advance,

That we had been given a wonderful chance.

We got some computers! They've got RAM and ROM!

Come, let me show you. This switch turns it on."

"The speakers use sound bytes, so we can hear,

With spoken directions, our answers are clear.

The monitor is what we call that TV,

It shows us the software that we want to see.

The software is what we call all our programs,

The mouse is what's used to give it commands!

It's kept on a mouse pad – we move it around

And highlight the icons we want to be found."

"There's also a touchpad to use with our hands

Instead of the mouse, to give our commands.

The icons are pictures of things we can do,

We push mouse's buttons to select a few.

We press on the left side for what we will use,

And sometimes the right to see what we can choose.

So, Rosie, I think that you'll play with this mouse,

And be very happy you did leave your house!"

"But what of the spiders?" asked Rosie with dread.

"I know that you warned us that we'd use a web."

Ms. Eddy smiled gently, and then shook her head,

"I don't think you listened to all that I said.

The web is the Internet, where we'll engage

In writing our news on the web's new school page.

We call it a web, for all schools come together

And share our ideas – we are linked with each other.

We'll type in our letters and tell what we've done."

Ms. Eddy then added, "We'll have lots of fun!"

Upcoming Events

Today:
• Visiting Author Assembly-Sherrill Cannon for grades K-3 at 2:30pm in cafeteria
Friday:
• Super Hero Day - Dress up like a super Hero!
Inter-school e-Mail Exchange

"I feel so much better. I'm happy now, too,"

Said Rosemary, then to her mother, "Thank you.

I think you can go now, I've nothing to fear,

I can't wait to use this computer right here!"

"It's great and I love it!" her mother exclaimed.

"There's only one question that's left to explain:

Why just for girls? Why only 'female'?"

Ms. Eddy just smiled and replied, "I said e-mail!"

ACKNOWLEDGEMENTS AND THANKS!

Thanks again to my awesome publisher, SBPRA, especially Robert, Lynn and Kait

And also Suzann, Shaina, Roger, Kim, Lee, Jeanine, Felicia, Ellen, & Denise,

Thanks to my Jr. Reviewers: Olivia, Cassie & Addie

Shout-out to my special Kids & Fans: Alyssa, Aolani, Ashlyn, Cameron, Daisy, Eliana, Kallista, Kathy, Jaden, Maddie, Selene, & Tristan

Thank you to those who help me share my books: Barbara, Donna, Jean, Julian, Julie, Kristen, Lorilyn, Pat, Rosalie, Rose, Susan, Tertia, & Tosha

Shout out to St. Katharine Drexel School for sharing photos of the computer lab – and to Loretta Gordish for sharing her computer expertise. Thank you to Buckingham Elementary School for suggesting the name for Rosemary's school!

Thanks to my family: Kim, KC, Christy, Kell, Steph, Kerry, John, Cailin, Paulo, Megan

In loving memory of Mary L. Gault and Jolie Voulopos ... Caring lives & sharing love!

SPECIAL NOTES FROM SHERRILL:

Can you find the covers of my other books in this book? (Peter and the Whimper-Whineys, The Magic Word, Gimme-Jimmy, Manner-Man, My Fingerpaint Masterpiece)

Do you recognize any of the characters from those books?

Are you a good listener? Does your teacher help you when you misunderstand something? Were you able to figure out the clues for the mouse, spider and female?

Do you have a computer in your classroom at school? Do you have one at home? Do you know how to use it?

Can you find these computer terms in the book: RAM, ROM, speakers, sound bytes, monitor, software, icons, mouse, touchpad, Internet, e-mail.

Are you afraid of mice and spiders? Why?

All of Sherrill S. Cannon's books are available at http://sbpra.com/curejm where 50% of the cost of the books goes to the CureJM Foundation to help find a cure for Juvenile Myositis, an incurable children's disease, and also at http://sbpra.com/imbullyfree.

Please consider these other award winning books by Sherrill S. Cannon:

Website: www.sherrillcannon.com

My Fingerpaint Masterpiece deals with perspective, perception and self-esteem as a child fingerpaints artwork in class, and later discovers it as part of the town's Art Contest. It has won a 2014 Readers' Favorite Gold Medal in Children's K-3, as well as their Illustrations Award, and also a Children's Literary Classics Seal of Approval and a Pinnacle Achievement Award.

ISBN 978-1-62857-288-9 - $12.50

Winner of ten awards: Winner of the 2014 CLIPP Principals' Award, the KART Kids Book List, the Reviewers Choice Award, the Los Angeles Book Festival, a Global eBook Silver Medal; as well as a 2013 Readers Favorite Silver Medal, National Indie Excellence Finalist, a Pinnacle Achievement Award, and H.M. in the London Book Fair and Rebecca's Reads Awards. Manner-Man is a Superhero who helps children cope with bullies, and teaches them how to look within themselves for their own superhero.

ISBN 978-1-62212-478-7 - $12.50

Winner of five awards: the 2013 Global eBook Silver Medal, Indie Excellence Finalist and Reader Views Finalist Awards as well as the 2012 Readers Favorite Silver Medal Award and the 2012 Pinnacle Achievement Winner Award

Gimme-Jimmy is about how a bully learns to share. His "New Polite Rule" helps him learn to make friends.

ISBN 978-1-61897-267-5 - $13.00

Winner of six awards: the 2011 Readers Favorite Gold Medal, 2011 Pinnacle Achievement Award Winner, 2011 Global Finalist Award, 2012 Reader Views Second Place, 2012 International Book Awards Finalist, and 2012 Next Generation Indie Finalist.

Elisabeth needs to learn *The Magic Word* "please", and to use it every day. Please and Thank you are words that everyone needs to use!

ISBN 978-1-6096-909-3 - $12.50

Winner of the 2011 Readers Favorite Bronze Medal and the 2011 USA Best Books Finalist Award

Peter and the Whimper-Whineys helps parents cope with whining, disguised as a fun story. Peter is a rabbit who whines all the time, and might have to join the Whimper-Whineys.

ISBN 978-1-60911-517-**3** - $13.00

Winner of the 2011 Readers Favorite Silver Award and the 2011 Indie Excellence Finalist Award.

Santa's Birthday Gift includes Santa in the Christmas story.

(After reading a story of the nativity to my granddaughter, she asked

"But where's Santa?")

ISBN 978-1-60860-824-9 - $11.50

CPSIA information can be obtained at www.ICGtesting.com
Printed in the USA
BVIW12n0437160415
396295BV00005B/20